The Not-So-Tiny Tales of
Simon Seahorse

Simon Says

By Cora Reef
Illustrated by Liam Darcy

LITTLE SIMON

New York London Toronto Sydney New Delhi

LITTLE SIMON

An imprint of Simon & Schuster Children's Publishing Division

1230 Avenue of the Americas, New York, New York 10020

First Little Simon paperback edition December 2021

Copyright © 2021 by Simon & Schuster, Inc.

Also available in a Little Simon hardcover edition

All rights reserved, including the right of reproduction in whole or in part in any form. LITTLE SIMON is a registered trademark of Simon & Schuster, Inc., and associated colophon is a trademark of Simon & Schuster, Inc. For information about special discounts for bulk purchases, please contact Simon & Schuster Special Sales at 1-866-506-1949 or business@simonandschuster.com.

The Simon & Schuster Speakers Bureau can bring authors to your live event. For more information or to book an event contact the Simon & Schuster Speakers Bureau at 1-866-248-3049 or visit our website at www.simonspeakers.com.

Designed by Leslie Mechanic

The text of this book was set in Causten Round.

Manufactured in the United States of America 1121 MTN

10 9 8 7 6 5 4 3 2 1

Library of Congress Cataloging-in-Publication Data

Names: Reef, Cora, author. | Darcy, Liam, illustrator.

Title: Simon says / by Cora Reef ; illustrated by Liam Darcy.

Description: First Little Simon paperback edition. | New York : Little Simon, an imprint of Simon & Schuster Children's Publishing Division, 2021. | Series: The not-so-tiny-adventures of Simon Seahorse ; 1 | Audience: Ages 5-9. | Summary: Little Simon Seahorse likes to tell stories, and if some of them are embellished, it just makes for a better story; but when his lucky pearl disappears after sea-and-tell at Coral Grove Elementary, he and his friends have a real-life treasure to find—and of course it will become a super story to tell, one that hardly needs embellishment.

Identifiers: LCCN 2021008590 (print) | LCCN 2021008591 (ebook) | ISBN 9781665903677 (paperback) | ISBN 9781665903684 (hardcover) | ISBN 9781665903691 (ebook)

Subjects: LCSH: Sea horses—Juvenile fiction. | Pearls—Juvenile fiction. | Lost articles—Juvenile fiction. | Storytelling—Juvenile fiction. | Friendship—Juvenile fiction. | CYAC: Sea horses—Fiction. | Pearls—Fiction. | Lost and found possessions—Fiction. | Storytelling—Fiction. | Friendship—Fiction.

Classification: LCC PZ7.1.R4423 Si 2021 (print) | LCC PZ7.1.R4423 (ebook) | DDC [Fic]—dc23

LC record available at https://lccn.loc.gov/2021008590

LC ebook record available at https://lccn.loc.gov/2021008591

Contents

A Good-Morning Story

"Simon! Hurry down for breakfast or you're going to be late for school!"

Simon could hear his dad calling up to him, but he still had a few more plates to comb. He wanted to make sure they looked perfect for sea-and-tell today. There, that looked right!

"Hi, Simon!" someone called from outside.

Simon peered out his window. It was his orca pal, Walter. Simon waved to him.

"Have a good day at school!" Walter said, and swam away. It took a minute for him to entirely disappear. He was twenty feet long, after all.

After gathering up his school-work, Simon glanced around for his lucky pearl. He couldn't wait to show it off to his classmates.

 It had a blue mark on one side that reminded Simon of the color of the ocean when the sun shone through. Now . . . where was it? Simon checked under his sponge bed and inside his seashell closet.

No luck. He burrowed his snout into his clamshell toy chest and—success!

He knew that he would have to come up with a great story about how he'd gotten the pearl. Everyone knew Simon Seahorse loved to tell a tale, and they looked forward to hearing his stories. Well, *most* everyone did.

Simon tucked the pearl into his backpack. Then he quickly swam downstairs. The kitchen seemed even more crowded than usual. And that was saying a lot because Simon had eleven brothers and sisters! Simon had to eat his kelp pancakes while floating *next* to the table.

"I was starting to think you'd swum up to the surface!" Simon's dad said with a smile.

"Well, you'll never believe what *actually* happened," Simon said. "A huge orca peeked through my window and sang me a good-morning song! Then I couldn't find my lucky pearl.

I searched high and low, from sea to ...
sea, and when I had almost given up
hope ..."

"Did you find it?" Simon's youngest
brother, Earl, asked eagerly.

"I   found   it!"   said   Simon
triumphantly.

Simon's oldest sister, Kya, had been bouncing a bubble on her head. She was training for bubble ball tryouts. But she suddenly stopped. "An orca *sang* you a good-morning song?" she asked, her eyes narrowed.

"Well," Simon began, "he did say good morning, but it wasn't a song. But if he *had* sung a song, it would have sounded like this!" Simon lowered his voice and broke into his version of a whale song. He did a little dance as he sang.

When he was done, his siblings clapped and cheered.

Kya laughed. "We don't call you 'Simon Says' for nothing!"

Simon smiled. It was true that his siblings called him that. "You can't beat a good story!" he said cheerfully. "Or a good song," he added.

"All right, everyone," Mr. Seahorse said. "It's getting late."

As his brothers and sisters swam out of the house, Simon gulped down the rest of his breakfast. Then he grabbed his backpack and checked to make sure everything was inside.

Oceanography homework?

Check.

Lucky pearl?

Check.

Glitter sand? Check. You never knew when you were going to need a little bit of glitter!

Simon put his backpack on and hurried outside.

At the corner of Seaweed Lane, his best friend, an octopus named Olive, was waiting for him.

"There you are!" Olive said. She checked the watches on each of her pink arms. "Come on. I don't want to ruin my perfect attendance record!"

They swam across the street and hopped into the current that would take them to school.

"So tell me what happened *this* morning," Olive said with a knowing smile.

"You'll never believe it. There was a huge orca outside my window!" Simon began. Then he launched into the rest of his incredible tale as they swam to school.

Amazing Crab Facts

The current brought Simon and Olive to Coral Grove Elementary just in time. They swam past the younger students on the lower levels of the reef and up toward Ms. Tuttle's classroom.

Simon slid into his usual seat next to Olive and waved to his friends Lionel and Nix.

"Good morning!" said Ms. Tuttle, a sea turtle. "I know you're all excited about sea-and-tell today." She stretched her neck to peer around the room. "Let's see. Who should go first?"

Simon quickly raised his fin, but Ms. Tuttle turned to Cam, a crab who was sitting in the front row. "Why don't we start from the front of the room this time. Cam?"

Cam got up from his seat with a big crabby smile. He scuttled sideways to the front of the classroom and proudly held up a book. "This is my favorite book. It's called *100 Interesting Facts about Crabs*. It has one hundred interesting facts about crabs."

"Could you share one of your favorite crab facts with us?" Ms. Tuttle asked.

Cam shook his head. "I don't think I can pick only one." Then he opened to the first page and began reading *all* one hundred facts about crabs.

Simon thought the first few were interesting. He had no idea there were over five thousand kinds of crabs in the ocean! Or that crabs have an exoskeleton that protects them. But while Cam's facts were cool, they weren't exactly a story. Weren't they supposed to *sea-and-tell* a story?

Finally, Cam finished his book . . .
just as some of the students were
starting to doze off.

"Thank you," Ms. Tuttle said as Cam
scurried back to his seat. "DeeDee?
It's your turn."

DeeDee, a guppy, showed off a sea-
glass necklace from her grandmother.

After that Lionel shared a drawing he'd done of his whole clown fish family.

Simon wiggled in his seat. He couldn't wait for his turn.

"Nix, do you want to go next?" Ms. Tuttle called out.

Nix, an eel, slithered to the front of the room. Her tail was glowing like it always did when she was nervous or excited.

"This is the coolest thing I own!" she said as she held up a shark's tooth. Everyone stared at it in awe.

"Where did you get that?" Lionel asked.

"Did you swim all the way to Shark Point and meet a shark and–" Simon began, ready to come up with something fantastic.

Nix laughed and shook her head. "My mom got it for me," she said. "Honestly, I've never even *seen* a shark."

The whole class sighed with disappointment.

Next it was Olive's turn. She headed to the front of the room holding a shell in each arm.

"I thought we were only supposed to bring *one* thing today," Cam pointed out.

"I did," Olive said. "I brought my talent." Then she started juggling the shells with all eight of her arms.

Even Simon was impressed, and he'd seen her practice lots of times. But, still, he wondered where all the stories were.

The students cheered as Olive headed back to her seat.

Ms. Tuttle scanned the room. "Simon? It's your turn!"

Simon took a deep breath, held his lucky pearl tight, and headed to the front of the room. It was time for his tale!

Sea-and-Tell

"This is my lucky pearl," Simon began. "See the little blue mark on its side? It reminds me of when the sunlight shines through the water."

No one seemed very impressed. In fact, a couple kids were gazing longingly out at the playground.

Simon hoped his story about the pearl would capture everyone's interest.

"But let me tell you all how I got this special pearl. I was out exploring Urchin Alley one day when a seal swam up to me."

The class gasped. They were all paying attention now. Seals rarely visited Coral Grove.

"The seal told me he was lost," Simon went on, "so I helped him find his way to Seal Cove. On the way back to my house, I spotted something shiny in a cave.

I reached for it and realized it wasn't a cave—it was a *shark's mouth*! The pearl fell out and I caught it. Then I swam as fast as I could back home. And ever since then, this has been my lucky pearl."

There was a long, wide-eyed silence.

"Thank you, Simon," Ms. Tuttle said finally. "That was quite a story!"

"I can't believe you've been to Seal Cove!" Nix said, her tail glowing again.

"I can't believe you reached into a shark's mouth!" cried Lionel.

But Cam was shaking his head. "There's no way that's true," he declared.

"I thought this was 'sea-and-tell a story,'" Simon admitted. "So I told a story."

Ms. Tuttle smiled. "That's okay! Cam, we know you like facts. And, Simon, we know you like stories. And both are perfectly acceptable for 'sea-and-tell.' Thank you for sharing them with us!"

Just then, the bell rang for recess.

"All right, everyone," Ms. Tuttle said. "We'll finish up sea-and-tell later. You can go put your special items away."

Simon tossed his pearl into the front pocket of his backpack. Then he swam over to Olive, who was carefully packing her shells away in a special box.

"That was some great juggling," Simon told her.

"Thanks," Olive said. "That was a great story."

Together, they swam out of the classroom and along the reef. Below, the playground was already echoing with shrieks and laughter.

"Race you to the swings?" Simon asked.

Olive grinned. "Last one there is a rotten fish egg!" she cried.

Simon Says

Simon and Olive's race to the swings ended in a tie. They both groaned with disappointment.

"I'll win next time. You'll see!" Olive said.

"No way," Simon told her. "I might be small, but I'm quick."

Both friends laughed.

Nix slid up to them. "Lionel and I are starting up a game of tag," she said. "Do you two want to play?"

Before either of them could answer, Cam scuttled over. "I bet Simon would rather daydream and make up more stories," he said. "Right, Simon Says?"

"Why are you calling him that?" Olive asked.

"Because," Cam said, "Simon *says* a lot."

Simon laughed. "I sure do say a lot! You probably would too if you had eleven brothers and sisters. In fact, that's what my siblings call me!"

Cam narrowed his eyes. "Do you really have such a big family?" he asked. "Or is that another one of your stories?"

"He *does* have that many brothers and sisters," Olive said defensively.

Then she turned to Nix and said, "We'll play tag next time, okay?"

Nix nodded and slithered off to invite DeeDee to play instead.

"Come on, Simon," Olive said, still glaring at Cam. "Let's go check out the sandcastle."

The sandcastle was Simon's favorite spot on the playground. But as they swam up to the top, Simon couldn't help thinking about what Cam had said.

"Do you think I tell too many stories?" he asked Olive.

"Of course not," Olive assured him. "Cam's just being crabby."

Simon nodded. Olive was right, he told himself.

The two friends peered out over the playground. Down below, the other kids looked like tiny shrimp.

"Wow. You can see the whole ocean from up here! I think I even see a spotted eagle ray over there," Simon said.

Olive smiled. "I'm not sure about that spotted eagle ray, but see if you

can *spot* me as I beat you back down to the playground!" And with that, Olive took off.

Olive and Simon spent the rest of recess chasing each other around. By the time they headed back to class, the last of Simon's worries had floated away.

The Missing Pearl!

When school was over, Simon rode the current home while Olive headed to the village library where her mother worked.

As Simon passed Barnacle Bakery, the current felt bumpier than usual. Simon gripped his backpack tighter, his thoughts miles away.

He was imagining the story he'd tell his family when they asked about sea-and-tell. Pretty soon he was acting it out, pretending that his backpack was a shield against the light rays of evil eels.

At home, Simon found all his brothers and sisters packed into the kitchen doing homework. Or at least, Simon *thought* they were all there. In a family of twelve kids, it was hard to keep track.

"How was school, Simon?" his dad asked as he stirred a large pot of kelp spaghetti on the stove.

"Good!" Simon said. "Wait until you hear what happened during sea-and-tell."

He reached into the front pocket of his backpack for his lucky pearl. But the pocket was empty.

Uh-oh.

Simon rushed into the living room and emptied out his backpack on the floor. Maybe he'd put the pearl in a different pocket by accident. But even after he'd turned his bag inside out, the pearl was nowhere to be found.

His siblings were still laughing and chatting when he swam back into the kitchen.

"What's wrong?" his dad asked when he saw the glum look on Simon's face.

"I can't find my lucky pearl!" Simon exclaimed.

"Maybe an orca appeared and whisked it away," Kya suggested with a laugh. Then she saw Simon's expression. She stopped laughing. "When did you last see it?"

"I put it in my backpack right after sea-and-tell," Simon said.

"Are you sure you didn't take it out again?" Mr. Seahorse asked.

Simon shook his head. "No, I didn't want to risk losing it."

"Maybe someone stole it!" Earl cried.

Simon frowned. Could someone in his class have taken

his pearl? No way. Simon couldn't imagine anyone doing that—not even Cam.

"It must have fallen out of my backpack," Simon decided. "I need to go look for it!"

Simon's dad shook his head. "It's getting dark, and dinner is almost ready."

"But–"

"You can go look tomorrow," his dad said. Then he winked. "Who knows, you might even find a good story along the way."

Simon nodded, but his chest felt tight. "I hope so," he said.

No Luck
at All

That night, Simon had trouble falling asleep. And it wasn't only because Earl was snoring like a walrus right next to him. Simon couldn't stop thinking about his lucky pearl.

Maybe the pearl wasn't exactly *lucky*. Despite what Simon had told his class, it hadn't come from a shark's mouth.

But Simon's dad had given Simon the pearl for his last birthday, which made it just as special. It couldn't be gone!

Fortunately, Simon knew he'd be seeing Olive in the morning. She'd know what to do. With that comforting thought in his head, Simon finally drifted off to sleep.

In the morning, Simon woke up early and rushed to comb his plates and pack for school.

"Good luck!" Simon's dad said as he handed Simon a slice of kelp toast for the road.

Simon kept his eyes on the ground all the way to Seaweed Lane, but there was no sign of his pearl. At the corner, he found Olive working on four crossword puzzles at once.

"Simon!" Olive said, surprised to see him. "You're here early today!"

"I need your help," he said. Then he told her about the missing pearl.

"That's terrible!" Olive said as they hopped into the current to school. "All right, we need a plan of action.

First, we'll search your desk at school.
Then we'll look around the—"

"Wait!" Simon cried. He grabbed
one of Olive's arms and pulled her out
of the current.

"Simon, what are you doing?" Olive
asked.

"Look!" He pointed to something
shining in the seaweed below. "My
pearl!"

Together, they swam down to get a better look. But as they got closer, Simon's excitement faded. It wasn't a pearl at all. It was a nautilus shell glinting in the light.

"I'm sorry, Simon," Olive said. "Come on. Let's get back in the current and keep searching."

The two friends kept an eye out all the way to school, but there were no pearls in sight.

At Coral Grove Elementary, they hurried up to Ms. Tuttle's room.

They checked Simon's desk, around
the classroom, and even in the trash.
But the pearl was nowhere to be found.

As the other kids started to arrive,
Simon began to lose hope.

"Don't worry," Olive told him. "We haven't checked the playground yet. And if we don't find it by this afternoon, we'll search along the current again."

Simon blinked. *The current.* He thought back to his ride home from school yesterday. He'd been acting out a story to tell his family, swinging his backpack around. What if he'd swung it so hard that the pearl had fallen out?

"Oh no," Simon said with a groan.

"What is it?" Olive asked.

Simon quickly explained his idea about what might have happened. "If I hadn't been acting out a story, the pearl never would have fallen out!"

Olive shook her head. "Even if you did lose your pearl that way, it was an accident. Your stories aren't to blame."

But suddenly Simon wasn't so sure.

The Meeting of the Tides

Simon had a hard time focusing that morning. During a spelling quiz, he accidentally added a y to the word "anemone." And his mind kept wandering during oceanography. All he could think about was his lucky pearl. Where could it be? Would he ever see it again?

At snack time, Lionel swam over. "Simon," he said, "is it true you lost the pearl you brought in for sea-and-tell yesterday?"

"Yes," Simon said with a sigh.

"Ooh," said Nix, her tail lighting up. "I bet there's an exciting story behind that!"

But for once, Simon didn't feel like telling one of his stories. So he only sighed again and said, "Not really." Then he put away his bag of kelp chips, his appetite suddenly gone.

During recess, Simon and Olive began searching the playground.

Pretty soon, the whole class was looking around for the pearl. Simon noticed that even Cam, who was pretending *not* to look, was keeping an eye out.

By the end of recess, they'd found a few loose buttons, a lost hat, and an old toy boat, but no pearl.

Simon thanked his classmates for their help. But he still felt disappointed.

Luckily, Olive had agreed to keep looking for the pearl after school. So when the last bell rang, she and Simon headed toward the village.

They needed to let Olive's mom know they'd be out searching for the pearl.

When they arrived at the library to tell Mrs. Octopus about their afternoon plans, she frowned.

Uh-oh. Was she not going to let them go?

"A pearl?" she asked. "Hmm, I am fairly certain I overheard someone talking about a pearl. Or *maybe* it was something that happened in a book they were returning...."

"Mom, think hard!" Olive said urgently. "Do you remember who was talking about it?"

"Why don't you check Sandy's Candy Shop next door?" Olive's mom suggested. "I *think* the conversation was happening outside."

"Thanks, Mrs. Octopus!" Simon shouted.

He and Olive hurried to Sandy's Candy Shop. Normally, they'd spend their time eyeing the different types of kelp candy and deciding which ones to try. But today, they had a mission.

KELP PUFFS

KELP
CHEWIES

MELTY KELP MIN

"Hi, Sandy!" Simon called when they entered.

"Hi, kids," said Sandy, a stingray. "What can I do for you today? We have some new flavors of sour kelp straws in. Or perhaps a kelpmallow?"

"Actually," said Olive, "we're looking for a very special pearl. Did you hear anyone talking about that yesterday?"

Sandy thought for a moment. Suddenly, her face brightened.

"Why, yes! I think I did!" she said. "Someone definitely handed a pearl they found to Mr. Green.

They said that because of the meeting of the tides yesterday, lots of things had blown away or gotten lost, and that perhaps the pearl belonged to . . . hmm, I can't remember who it might have belonged to."

"The meeting of the tides?" Olive asked.

"Oh yes," said Sandy. "When two tides meet, it creates huge waves that reach all the way down to us. That's why the current was so bumpy yesterday."

Olive started to ask another question, but Simon jumped in.

"We've got to find Mr. Green!" he said. He grabbed one of Olive's arms and called, "Thank you, Sandy!" as they rushed out of the store.

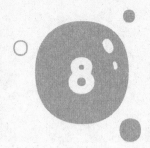

All Aboard
the Turtle Trolley

Mr. Green was the Coral Grove turtle trolley. If a sea creature ever needed to get somewhere that a current couldn't take them, they just had to hail Mr. Green. Or wait at a trolley stop.

"Where are we going to find Mr. Green?" Simon wondered.

Olive thought for a moment.

"The trolley schedule!" she said. The friends hurriedly swam over to the town's trolley stop, where a schedule was posted.

Using a tentacle, Olive scanned the schedule. "Hmm, 3:32 p.m. means Mr. Green should be right . . . here."

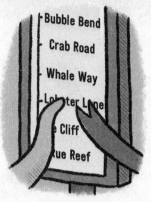

Bubble Bend
Crab Road
Whale Way
Lobster Lane
e Cliff
ue Reef

"Whale Way," Simon read aloud. And thanks to his friend Walter, he knew just how to get there.

Simon and Olive hopped into the current. A few minutes later, they arrived at Whale Way.

Olive looked in awe at the humongous whales who were swimming around. But there was no sign of Mr. Green.

Just then, Simon spotted a large black-and-white whale with a bull's-eye circle on one fin. It was Walter!

"Walter!" Simon cried. "Do you know where Mr. Green is?"

"Oh, hi, Simon!" cried Walter cheerfully. "Mr. Green should be at our trolley stop, three bunches of seaweed over."

"Thanks!" Simon said. "I'll come visit you tomorrow!" And with that, he and Olive swam off.

They arrived at the trolley stop just in time. Mr. Green was about to swim away.

"Mr. Green!" cried Simon.

"Hello, kids," said the turtle. "What can I do for you today?"

"We're looking for Simon's lucky pearl," Olive said.

"Yes. My lucky pearl that has a blue mark on one side. Have you seen it?" Simon asked.

Mr. Green nodded. "I believe I have," he said. "Hop on, kids."

"Olive, I can go by myself if you don't want to come," said Simon. He felt bad dragging her all over Coral Grove looking for his pearl.

"And miss the ending to this story?"
Olive asked. "I don't think so!"

Simon smiled. "All right, Mr. Green.
Let's go!"

Shipwreck Station

Mr. Green swam down, down, down. The water got colder. The light started to fade. Where were they going?

Suddenly, the turtle stopped.

"Where—where are we?" asked Olive.

Looking around, Simon saw all sorts of shiny things glinting in the bit of light that shone through the water.

"Shipwreck Station," Mr. Green replied. "There are wonderful treasures down here, and Atlanta cares for them all."

"Atlanta?" asked Simon.

Suddenly, something swam toward them. Simon couldn't tell what it was because it was glowing so brightly. The glow got closer and closer. And brighter and brighter. When it arrived, Simon saw that the glow was . . . a fish!

"This is Atlanta!" said Mr. Green.

"Wow," Simon said. "I love your light."

Atlanta laughed. "Well, thank you. I'm a lantern fish!" he explained. "I have bioluminescence. It means I

can glow. And I need that to see all the wonderful treasures down here."

Simon realized that this must be what made Nix's tail glow too.

"Let me show you around!" Atlanta offered.

Mr. Green cleared his throat. "Atlanta, I'm sure these kids would love for you to give them a tour of Shipwreck Station, but I have to be back in Coral Grove for a pickup. Do you have that pearl I gave you yesterday?"

"Oh yes! The one with the beautiful blue mark on it?" said Atlanta.

Simon's heart beat fast. "Yes!" he cried. "It's my lucky pearl!"

Atlanta smiled and reached into something that looked like a treasure chest behind him. He took something out. Then Simon saw that in his fins, Atlanta was holding a pearl. He handed it to Simon.

Simon turned it around in his own fins until he saw the blue mark. It was his lucky pearl. And he had it back.

A Perfect Ending

The next day, Simon met Olive at the corner of Seaweed Lane, as always.

"I'm just so happy my pearl is back safe and sound," Simon told Olive as they headed to school.

The day before, Mr. Green had explained to Simon and Olive that he had found the pearl swirling in the water after the current finally stopped going wild. He thought Atlanta might be able to identify the pearl and figure out who its owner was.

Simon had promised Atlanta that the next time he found a treasure, he'd bring it down to Shipwreck Station. Now he and Olive just *had* to explore Coral Grove more!

And Simon had realized something else. It *wasn't* his storytelling that had lost him his pearl, after all. It was the current. And now he had his lucky pearl back.

Finally, Simon and Olive arrived at Coral Grove Elementary. Simon was so happy that he barely noticed Cam Crab lingering outside the school. Even for a crab, Cam looked a bit down.

"Is everything okay?" Simon asked Cam.

Cam paused, clearly considering whether he should answer Simon. Then he shook his head. "I didn't have time to finish my art project, and it looks really . . . bad."

Simon had his own art project in his backpack. He loved art and had finished the project ahead of time.

"Can I see it?" Simon asked.

Cam hesitated again. Then he pulled something out of his backpack. It was a painting of himself with all his friends gathered around him.

"I think it looks great!" Simon said. "I love what you've done with the colors. I always wanted . . . uh . . . purple plates," said Simon, peering closer at what he *thought* was himself.

"I wanted to add one more thing to really make it shine," Cam admitted. "But I couldn't figure out what, and then . . . I ran out of time."

Shine made Simon think of something: his glitter sand! He rummaged through his backpack and then pulled it out.

"It's so . . . sparkly!" Cam said, admiring it.

"Go ahead and use some, if you want," Simon said, offering the bottles to Cam.

Cam selected a multicolored glitter
sand. He sprinkled it in little areas
around his painting. Then he, Simon,
and Olive stood back.

"What do you think?" asked Simon.

"I love it!" Cam said with a huge
smile. Well, a huge smile for a crab.
"Thank you," he said to Simon. "Hey,
did you ever find your lucky pearl?"

Simon and Olive looked at each other and grinned.

"Yes," Simon said, "and you'll never believe how we found it. I'll tell you the whole story at the playground later."

And with that, Olive, Cam, and Simon swam into school.

SIMON'S STORY

There once lived a seahorse named Simon. He had an amazing set of plates, and he was the bravest seahorse in Coral Kingdom. Simon had a pearl that brought him luck wherever he went and that even granted wishes! Once, Simon wished that he could be a golden seahorse. Another time, he wished his friend Olive would never be late to school no matter how late she was actually running. One day, Simon's pearl was

stolen by a giant squid! Simon swam after the squid. But then he had an idea. He wished he could be a giant seahorse, and suddenly he became the biggest creature in the ocean! He took his lucky pearl back and told the giant squid never to come to Coral Kingdom again.

THE END

Here's a peek at Simon's next big adventure!

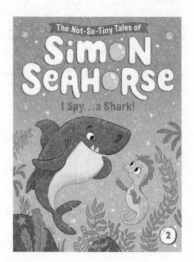

"So, Koto the shark kept swimming," Simon Seahorse said. "He was sure he was lost now."

Simon glanced around at his family to make sure everyone was paying attention. His siblings and

An excerpt from *I Spy . . . a Shark!*

his dad were spread out on bubble chairs in the living room.

They'd finished dinner and were now passing around a platter of kelp-chip cookies. Everyone was listening to Simon's story with wide eyes.

"Oh no!" said his youngest brother, Earl. "What is the shark going to do?"

"Just then," Simon went on, "Koto came upon something he'd never seen before. It was a huge shipwreck with tons of treasures! There were piles of golden coins and sparkling silver statues."

An excerpt from *I Spy ... a Shark!*

Lulu, his second-youngest sibling, squealed with excitement. She loved anything shiny.

"Suddenly, a lantern fish named Atlanta came swimming out!" Simon cried.

"Oh!" Earl piped up. "Your friend Atlanta. You told us about him before."

Simon nodded and continued his story. "Atlanta knew the ocean better than anyone. And luckily for Koto, he knew exactly how to get back to Shark Point. So Atlanta showed Koto the way home, and the shark lived happily ever after. The end!"

An excerpt from *I Spy ... a Shark!*